Dear Parents:

Congratulations! Your child is taking the first steps on an exciting journey. The destination? Independent reading!

STEP INTO READING® will help your child get there. The program offers five steps to reading success. Each step includes fun stories and colorful art or photographs. In addition to original fiction and books with favorite characters, there are Step into Reading Non-Fiction Readers, Phonics Readers and Boxed Sets, Sticker Readers, and Comic Readers—a complete literacy program with something to interest every child.

Learning to Read, Step by Step!

Ready to Read   Preschool–Kindergarten
• big type and easy words • rhyme and rhythm • picture clues
For children who know the alphabet and are eager to begin reading.

Reading with Help   Preschool–Grade 1
• basic vocabulary • short sentences • simple stories
For children who recognize familiar words and sound out new words with help.

Reading on Your Own   Grades 1–3
• engaging characters • easy-to-follow plots • popular topics
For children who are ready to read on their own.

Reading Paragraphs   Grades 2–3
• challenging vocabulary • short paragraphs • exciting stories
For newly independent readers who read simple sentences with confidence.

Ready for Chapters   Grades 2–4
• chapters • longer paragraphs • full-color art
For children who want to take the plunge into chapter books but still like colorful pictures.

STEP INTO READING® is designed to give every child a successful reading experience. The grade levels are only guides; children will progress through the steps at their own speed, developing confidence in their reading. The F&P Text Level on the back cover serves as another tool to help you choose the right book for your child.

Remember, a lifetime love of reading starts with a single step!

Text copyright © 2023 by Amy K. Rosenthal GST Exempt Family Trust
Cover art and interior illustrations copyright © 2023 by Brigette Barrager

Written by Candice Ransom
Illustrations by Kaley McCabe

All rights reserved. Published in the United States by Random House Children's Books,
a division of Penguin Random House LLC, New York.

Step into Reading, Random House, and the Random House colophon are registered trademarks
of Penguin Random House LLC.

Visit us on the Web!
rhcbooks.com

Educators and librarians, for a variety of teaching tools, visit us at RHTeachersLibrarians.com

Library of Congress Cataloging-in-Publication Data
Names: Ransom, Candice F., author | McCabe, Kaley, illustrator | Barrager, Brigette, illustrator |
Rosenthal, Amy Krouse.
Title: Uni and the 100 treasures : an Amy Krouse Rosenthal book / written by Candice Ransom ;
illustrations by Kaley McCabe ; pictures based on art by Brigette Barrager.
Other titles: Uni and the one hundred treasures
Description: First edition. | New York : Random House Children's Books, 2023. |
Series: Uni the unicorn | Audience: Ages 4–6. | Summary: "Uni the unicorn sets out to help
the little girl collect 100 treasures to celebrate her 100th day at school." —Provided by publisher
Identifiers: LCCN 2022049412 (print) | LCCN 2022049413 (ebook) |
ISBN 978-0-593-65202-2 (trade) | ISBN 978-0-593-65200-8 (library binding) |
ISBN 978-0-593-65201-5 (ebook)
Subjects: CYAC: Unicorns—Fiction. | Friendship—Fiction. | Schools—Fiction. |
LCGFT: Picture books.
Classification: LCC PZ7.R1743 Uf 2023 (print) | LCC PZ7.R1743 (ebook) | DDC [E]—dc23

Printed in the United States of America
10 9 8 7 6 5 4 3 2 1

First Edition

This book has been officially leveled by using the F&P Text Level Gradient™ Leveling System.

UNI and the 100 Treasures

Uni the UNICORN

an Amy Krouse Rosenthal book
pictures based on art by Brigette Barrager

Random House New York

A note flies
into Uni's window.
It is from
the little girl.

Uni slides down
the rainbow to
the little girl's house.

"I am here!" says Uni.
"How can I help?"

"Tomorrow is the
100th day of school,"
the little girl says.
"I need to bring
one hundred things
to my class."

She shows Uni
some things
she has collected.

She has
marbles and hair clips.

She has building blocks,

stuffed bears,
and toy dinosaurs.

"I have fifty things.
I need fifty more!"
Uni's friend is
stuck.

"Did you look outside?"
Uni asks.

"What will be outside?"
the little girl asks.

"Treasures! Grab a bag!"
Uni says.

They walk to
an oak tree.

A squirrel hops
on a branch.
Down drop acorns!

"Treasures from this tree."
Uni puts ten acorns
in the bag.
"What else can we find?"
the little girl asks.

"Leaves!" Uni says.
They gather twelve
leaves.

"These are the prettiest,"
says the little girl.

Sixteen pinecones lay
under a pine tree.
"I like these,"
says the little girl.

Next, they go to
the creek.
They collect ten
green stones.

"My bag is getting full!"
Uni's friend is happy.
So is Uni.

A bird flies overhead.
One blue feather
floats to the ground.

"Treasure from the sky," says Uni.

The little girl counts
the things in her bag.
"Forty-nine," she says.
"I have fifty things
at home."

Uni adds the numbers.
"Fifty plus forty-nine
is ninety-nine."
"I need one more thing!"
says the little girl.

"How about another
rock or a leaf?"
Uni asks.
"No," says the little girl.
"The 100th thing
should be special."
She sounds sad.

Uni feels sad, too.
The little girl
has tried hard
to collect
one hundred treasures.

Uni sees a clam shell.

It is plain and gray.

It is not special.

But it could be.

Uni's magic horn taps
the clam.

The shell splits.

Uni gives the clam
to the little girl.
"Maybe this?"
says Uni.

The little girl opens
the plain gray shell.
Her face lights up!
"So pretty!"

Inside is a
round white pearl!

A real treasure
from nature!

Uni picks up the bag.
"We must go pack
   your one hundred things
   for school," says Uni.
"Because friends
   help each other."

The little girl hugs Uni.

"A good friend
is the best treasure
of all," she says.
Uni's horn glows.